Ian would like to dedicate this book to Cosmo Miller.

And David says:

For Petra, Filip and Darija

And to all you chickens out there, if you ever meet Nicholas....RUN!

GENTLY BENTLEY
by Ian Whybrow and David Melling

British Library Cataloguing in Publication Data
A catalogue record of this book is available
from the British Library.
ISBN 0 340 87561 5 (HB)
ISBN 0 340 87562 3 (PB)

First hardback edition published 2004
First paperback edition published 2005
10 9 8 7 6 5 4 3 2

Published by Hodder Children's Books
a division of Hodder Headline Limited
338 Euston Road London NW1 3BH

Originated by Dot Gradations Ltd, UK
Printed in China

# Gently Bentley

## Ian Whybrow • David Melling

Hodder
Children's
Books

A division of Hodder Headline Limited

Bentley was very fond of his squashy caterpillar.

You could **bash** it.

You could **crash** it.

It was fun to be **rough** with it.

But one day Bentley bit it and
the caterpillar went

bang!

After that it wasn't the same.

So off went Bentley to see Squeaky and Bun.
"Don't be upset," said Bun.

"We're sure to find
something else you can
play with," said Squeaky.

"Cars are fun," said Squeaky.
"Look, I'll show you."
Bentley tried pulling but the wheel fell off.

"Gently Bentley!" said Squeaky.
"Blow it!" said Bentley. "I'm much too
rough for cars!"

"Tennis is fun," said Bun.
"Look, I'll show you."

Bentley tried tennis but he couldn't get the hang of it.

"Gently Bentley!" said Bun.

"Blow it!" said Bentley. "I'm much too rough for bats and balls."

"How about a skipping rope?" said Squeaky.
"Look, I'll show you."

Bentley tried skipping but it was a bit too tangly.

"Gently Bentley!" said Squeaky and Bun.

"Blow it!" said Bentley.
"I'm much too rough for ropes!"

"We'll try one last thing," said Bun.
"Bricks are fun. Now watch carefully, and...
*Gently* Bentley. Squeaky and I will show you."

So Squeaky and Bun took the bricks out of the brick-buggy.

They built a beautiful tower; it was ever so tall.

"I can do a tower!"
said Bentley.

But **bang,** he knocked it over.

"Bother!" said Squeaky and Bun. "Bears are much too rough to play anything properly!"

"Sorry," said Bentley. "Let's go somewhere and play house."

"But I'm too tired to go looking for houses," grumbled Bun.
"Me too," said Squeaky.

"I know," said Bentley. "Get in the brick-buggy!"
So into the brick-buggy got Squeaky and Bun.

And "Brrrm!" went Bentley.

He crashed it and he bashed it.

Squeaky and Bun had to hold on tight!

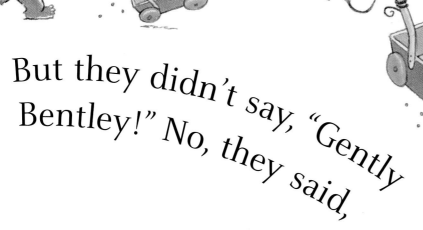

But they didn't say, "Gently Bentley!" No, they said,

"Wheeee!

Faster Bentley! This is fun!"

They bashed about till they found a box.
Bentley said, "If I give you my nice box can
I borrow your brick-buggy to play with?
Brick-buggies are just right for rough bears!"

"Of course you can borrow our brick-buggy,"
said Squeaky and Bun.
"Thank you! Hooray!" said Bentley and he
threw the brick-buggy up in the air.

"Gently Bentley!"
shouted Squeaky and Bun.

"Oh no!" said Bentley. "Was that too rough?"

But the brick-buggy didn't mind at all.

When it landed it landed just right!
"A house!" said Bentley and Squeaky and Bun.
Then Bentley played gently so they all had fun.